THE GOOSE IS GETTING FAT

By Michael Morpurgo
Illustrated by Sophie Allsopp

EGMONT

In memory of so many wonderful Christmases together:
For Edna, Mac, Seonaid and Stuart,
and for all their families since.

M.M.

EGMONT

We bring stories to life

First published by Egmont UK Limited in Great Britain 2012 in *Christmas Stories*
This edition published in 2013 by Egmont UK Limited,
The Yellow Building, 1 Nicholas Road, London W11 4AN

www.egmont.co.uk

Text copyright © Michael Morpurgo 2012
Illustrations copyright © Sophie Allsopp 2012

The moral rights of the author and illustrator have been asserted

ISBN 978 1 4052 6896 7

A CIP catalogue record for this title is available from the British Library

56507/1

Gertrude was a goose like any other goose. Hatched out in the orchard one drizzly morning in June, she spent those early weeks looking at the world from the warm sanctuary of her mother's all-enveloping softness. It might have come as a surprise to her to know that her mother was not a goose.

Of course Gertrude was convinced she was, and that was all that mattered; but in reality her mother was a rather ragged speckled hen. She was, however, the most pugnacious, the most jealous and possessive hen on the farm, and that was why Charlie's father had shut her up inside a coop with a vast goose egg and kept her there until something happened. Each day she had been lifted off and the egg sprinkled with water to soften the shell. The summer had been dry that year, and all the early clutches of goose eggs had failed. This was very probably the last chance they had of rearing a goose for Christmas.

There had always been a goose for Christmas Day, Charlie's father said – a goose reared on their own corn and in their own orchard. So he had picked out the nastiest, broodiest hen in the yard to guard the egg and to rear his Christmas goose, and Charlie had sprinkled the egg each day.

When Charlie and his father first spied the golden gosling scavenging in the long grass with the speckled black hen clucking close by, they raced each other up the lane to break the good news to Charlie's mother.

She pretended to be as happy about it **all as the**y were, but in her heart of hearts she had been **hoping** that there would be no goose to rear and pluck **that year.** The job she detested most was fattening the goo**se for** Christmas and then plucking it. The plucking took **her hours,** and the feathers flew everywhere, clouds **of them** – in her hair, down her neck. Her wrists and **fingers** ached with the work of it. But worst of all, sh**e could** not bear to look at the sweet, sad face she had **come to** know so well, hanging down over her **knee,** still smiling. She would willingly pluck a pheasant, a hen, even a woodcock; she **would** skin and gut a rabbit – anything but another goose.

Now Charlie's father was no fool and he knew his wife well enough to sense her disappointment. It was to soften the news, to console her and no doubt to persuade her again, that he suggested that Charlie might help this year. He had his arm round Charlie's shoulder, and that always made Charlie feel like a man.

"Charlie's almost ten now, lovely," he said. Charlie's father always called his mother 'lovely', and Charlie liked that. "Ten years old next January, and he'll be as tall as you next Christmas. He'll be taller than me before he's through growing. Just look at him, he's grown an inch since breakfast."

"I know Charlie's nearly ten, dear," she said. "I was there when he was born, remember?"

"Course you were, my lovely," Charlie's father said,

taking the drying-up cloth from her and sitting down at the kitchen table. "I've got a plan, see. I know you've never been keen on rearing the goose for Christmas, and Charlie and me have been thinking about it, haven't we, Charlie?"

Charlie hadn't a clue what his father was talking about, but he grinned and nodded anyway because it seemed the best thing to do.

"We thought that this year all three of us could look after the goose, you know, together like. Charlie boy can feed her up each day and drive her in each night. He can fatten her up for us. I'll kill her when the time comes – I know it seems a terrible thing to do, but what's got to be done has got to be done – and perhaps you wouldn't mind doing the little bit of plucking at the end for us. How would that be, my lovely?"

Charlie was
flattered by the
confidence his father
had placed in him
and his mother was,
as usual, beguiled
by both his Welsh
tongue and the
warmth of his smile.
And so it was that
Charlie came to rear
the Christmas goose.

The fluffy, flippered gosling was soon exploring every part of the orchard and soon outgrew her bad-tempered foster mother. The hen shadowed her for as long as she could. Then she gave up and went back to the farmyard.

The gosling turned into a goose, long and lovely and white. Charlie watched her grow. He would feed her twice a day, before and after school, with a little mixed corn. On fine autumn days he would sit with her in the orchard for hours at a time and watch her grazing under the trees. And he loved to watch her preening herself, her eyes closed in ecstasy as she curved her long neck and delved into the white feathers on her chest.

Charlie called the goose 'Gertrude' because she reminded him of his tall, lean Aunty Gertrude who always wore feathers in her hat in church. His aunt's nose was so imperial in shape and size that her neck seemed permanently stretched with the effort of seeing over it. But she was, for all that, immensely elegant and poised, so there could be no other name for the goose but Gertrude.

And Gertrude moved through her orchard kingdom with an air of haughty indifference and an easy elegance that sets a goose apart from all other fowl. To Charlie, however, Gertrude had more than this. She had the gentle charm and sweetness of nature that Charlie warmed to as the autumn months passed.

They harvested cider apples in late October, so Gertrude's peace was disturbed each day for over two weeks as they climbed the lichen-coated apple trees and shook until the apples rained down on the grass. Gertrude and Charlie stood side by side waiting for the storm to pass, and then Charlie moved in to gather up the apples and fill the sacks. Gertrude stood back like a foreman and cackled encouragement from a distance. Her wings were fully grown now, and in her excitement she would raise

herself to her full height,
open her great white wings,
stretch her neck, and beat the
air with wild enthusiasm.

"It's clapping, she is," said
Charlie's father from
high up in the tree.
"A grand bird. She's
growing well. Be fine by
Christmas if you look after
her. We've got plenty of
Bramley apples this year,
good for stuffing. Nothing like
apple stuffing in a Christmas
goose, is there, Charlie?"

The words fell like stones on Charlie's heart. As a farmer's son he knew that most of the animals on the farm went for slaughter. It was an accepted fact of life; neither a cause for sorrow nor rejoicing. Sick lambs, rescued piglets, ill suckling calves – Charlie helped to care for all of them and had already developed that degree of detachment that a farmer needs unless he is to be on the phone to the vet five times a day. But none of these animals were killed on the farm – they went away to be killed, and so he did not have to think about it. Charlie had seen his father shoot rats and pigeons and squirrels but that again was different, they were pests.

Now, for the first time, as he watched Gertrude patrolling behind the dung heap, he realised that she had only two months to live, that she would be killed, hung up, plucked, pulled, stuffed and cooked, and borne in triumph onto the table on Christmas Day. "Nothing like apple stuffing in a Christmas goose" – his father's words would not go away.

Gertrude lowered her head and hissed at an intruding gaggle of hens that flew up in a panic and scattered into the hedgerow. She raised her wings again and beat them in a dazzling display before resuming her dignified patrol. She was magnificent, Charlie thought, a queen among geese. At that moment he decided that Gertrude was not going to be killed for Christmas. He would simply not allow it to happen.

With the frosts and winds of November, the last of the leaves were blown from the trees and swirled round the farmyard. Then the winter rains came and piled them into soggy, mushy heaps against the hedgerows, clogging the ditches and filling the pot-holes. It was fine weather for a goose, though, and Gertrude revelled in the wildness of the winter winds. She stalked serenely through the leaves, her head held high against the wind and the rain, her feathers blown and ruffled.

Each day when Charlie got back from school he drove Gertrude in from the orchard to the safety of an empty calf pen. Foxes do come out on windy nights, and he did not want Gertrude taken by the fox any more than he wanted her carved up at Christmas. Before breakfast every morning Charlie opened the calf pen, and the two of them walked side by side out into the orchard where he emptied the scoop of corn into Gertrude's bowl. He talked to her all the while of the great master-plan he had dreamed up and how she must learn not to cackle too loudly.

"Won't be long now, Gerty," he said. "But if you make too much noise, you're done for. Your goose will be cooked, and that's for sure." But Gerty wasn't listening. She had found a leafy puddle and was busy drinking from it, dipping and lifting her head, dipping and lifting . . .

Until late November his father had not taken much interest in Gertrude's progress, but now with Christmas only six weeks away he was asking almost daily whether or not Gertrude would be fat enough in time.

"She'll do better on oats, Charlie," he said one breakfast. "And I think you ought to shut her up now, and I don't mean just at night. I mean all the time. This wandering about in the orchard is all very well, but she won't put on much weight that way. There won't be much left on her for us, will there? You leave her in the calf pen from now on and feed her up."

"She wouldn't like that," Charlie said. "You know she wouldn't. She likes her freedom. She'd pine away inside and lose weight." Charlie had his reasons for wanting to keep Gertrude out in the orchard by day.

"Charlie's right, dear," his mother said softly. "Of course you're both right, really." His mother was the perfect diplomat. "Gertrude will fatten up better inside, but it's lean meat we want, not fat. The more natural food she eats and the happier she is, the better she'll taste. My father used to say, 'A happy goose is a tender goose'. And anyway, there's only the three of us on Christmas Day, and Aunt Gertrude, of course. What would we do with a fifteen-pound goose?"

"All right, my lovely," said Charlie's father. "I know better than to argue when you and Charlie get together. But feed her on oats, Charlie, else there'll be nothing on her but skin and bone. And remember I have to kill her about a week before Christmas – a goose needs a few days to hang. And then you'll need a day or so for plucking and

dressing, won't you, lovely? I can smell it already," he said, closing his eyes and sniffing the air. "Goose and apple stuffing, roast potatoes, sprouts and chipolata sausages. Oh Christmas is coming and the goose is getting fat!"

The days rolled by into December, and Christmas beckoned. There was a Nativity play at school in which Charlie played Joseph. There were the endless shopping expeditions into town when Charlie dragged along behind his mother, who would never make up her mind about anything. Christmas with all its heady excitement meant little to Charlie that year for all he could think of was Gertrude. Again and again he went over the rescue plan in his mind until he was sure he had left nothing to chance.

December 16th was the day Charlie decided upon. It was a Saturday, so he would be home all day. But more important, that morning, Charlie knew his father would be out following the hunt five miles away at Dolton. He had asked Charlie if he wanted to go with him, but Charlie said he had to clean out Gertrude's pen. "It's a pity you can't come," said his father. "Lovely frosty morning. There'll be a fine scent."

Charlie watched from the farm gate until his father rattled off down the lane in the battered Land Rover. Then Charlie wasted no time. It was a long walk down to the river and he had to make a detour through the woods out of sight in case his mother spotted him.

Gertrude was waiting by the door of the calf pen as usual, impatient to get out into the orchard. But this morning she was not allowed to stop by her bowl of corn. Instead she was driven firmly out into the field beyond the orchard. She protested noisily, cackling and hissing, trying to get back by turning this way and that. But Charlie paid no attention. He banged his stick on the ground to keep her moving on. "It's for your own good, Gerty, you'll see," he said. "It has to be far away to be safe. It's a hiding place no one will ever find. No one goes there in the winter, Gerty. You'll be as safe as houses down there, and no one will eat you for Christmas. Next year you'll be too tough to eat anyway. They say a goose can live for forty years.

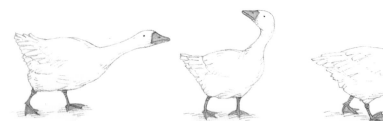

Think of that – not six months but forty years. So stop making a fuss, and walk on."

He talked to her all the way down through Watercress Field, into Little Wood and out into Lower Down. By the time they reached the marsh, Gertrude was exhausted and had stopped her cackling. Every gateway was a trial, with the puddles iced over. Try as she did, the goose could not keep her balance. She slithered and slipped across the ice until she found the ground rough and hard under her feet again. All the while the stick beat the ground behind her so that she could not turn around and go home.

The fishing hut stood only a few yards from the river, an ugly building, squat and corrugated, but ideal for housing a refugee goose.

In the last few days Charlie had moved out all the fishing tackle. He had laid a thick carpet of straw on the floor so that Gertrude would be warm and comfortable. In one corner was the old hip bath he had found in the attic. The bath was brim full of water and Charlie had hitched a ramp over the side. By the door was a feeding trough already full of corn. But Gertrude was not impressed by her new home. She walked straight to the darkest end of the hut and hissed angrily at Charlie. He rattled the trough to show her where the corn was, but the goose looked away disdainfully. Her whole routine had been rudely disturbed and all she wanted to do was to sulk.

"You'll be all right, Gerty," said Charlie. "But if you do hear anyone, don't start cackling. You've got food and water, and I'll be down to see you when I can. I can't come

too often. It's a long way and they might get suspicious."
Gertrude hissed at him once again and turned her head
away. "I love you too!" said Charlie, and he went out,
bolting the door firmly behind him.

Charlie ran back all the way home because he needed
to be breathless when he got there. His mother was just
finishing icing the cake when Charlie came bursting in
through the kitchen door. "She's gone. Gertrude's gone.
She's not in the orchard. She's not anywhere."

Charlie and his mother searched all that morning and through the afternoon until the frost came down with the darkness and forced them to stop. Of course they found no sign of Gertrude.

"I can't understand it," said Charlie's mother, as they broke the news to his father. "She's just vanished. There's no feathers and no blood."

"Well I can't believe it's a fox, anyway," said Charlie's father. "Not in broad daylight with a hunt just on the other side of the parish. She's in a hedge somewhere, laying an egg perhaps. They do that in winter sometimes, you know. She'll be back as soon as she gets hungry. It's a pity, though. She'll lose weight out in the cold."

Charlie's mother was upset. "We'll never find her if it snows. They've forecast snow tonight."

And that night the snow did come. Snow upon snow. When Charlie looked out of his bedroom window the next morning, the farm had been transformed. Every muddy lane and rusty roof was immaculate with snow. Charlie was out early, as usual, helping his father feed the bullocks before breakfast. Then, saying he wanted to look for Gertrude, he set off towards the river, carrying a bucket of corn.

Gertrude hissed as he opened the door of the fishing
hut, but when she saw who it was, she broke into an
excited cackle and opened her wings in pure delight.
She loved Charlie again. Charlie poured out the corn
and topped up the water in the hip bath. "So far, so good,
Gerty," he said. "Not so bad in here, is it? Better in here
than out. There's snow outside, but you'll be warm enough
in here. Father thinks you're laying an egg in
a hedge somewhere. Mother's worried sick about you.
I can't tell her until after Christmas, though, 'cos
she'd have to tell Father. But she'll understand,
and she'll make Father understand, too.
See you tomorrow, Gerty."

Every day for a week, Charlie trudged down through the snow to feed Gertrude. By this time both his mother and father had given up all hope of ever finding their Christmas goose. "It must have been a fox," his mother reflected sadly. "Gerty wouldn't just have walked off. But you'd think there would have been a tell-tale feather or two, wouldn't you? Don't be upset, Charlie."

Charlie had always found it easy to bring tears to his eyes and he did so now. "But she was my goose," he sniffed. "It was all my fault. I should have shut her up like Father said."

"Come on, Charlie," said his father, putting an arm round him. "We can't have all these tears over a goose, now can we? After all we were going to eat her, and have you ever heard of anyone crying over Christmas dinner?"

Charlie was proud of his tearful performance,
but was careful not to overdo it. "I'll be all right,"
he said manfully. "I'm going
to keep looking, though,
just in case."

One night, two days before Christmas, the wind changed from the north-east and rain came in from the west. By the morning, the snows had gone and the farm looked real and untidy again. Charlie could see the brook from his window. But instead of a gentle burbling stream, the brook had turned into a raging brown torrent rushing down towards the river.

The river! If the river burst its bank the fishing hut
would be under water, and Gertrude would be trapped
inside. She wasn't used to swimming. Her feathers would
be waterlogged and she would drown.

He dressed quickly and within minutes was running
down towards the river. As he opened the gate into
the marsh, he could see that the hut was completely
surrounded by water and that the door was wide open.

He splashed through the floods, praying that he would find Gertrude still alive and safe. But Gertrude wasn't even there. The trough and the straw floated in a foot of muddy water, but of Gertrude there was neither sound nor sight.

Somehow the door had opened and Gerty had escaped. He must have forgotten to bolt it, and the force of the flood water had done the rest. Now Gertrude was out there somewhere in the floods on her own. This time she had really escaped and when Charlie cried he really meant it, and the tears flowed uncontrollably.

Charlie spent the rest of the day searching the banks of the river for Gertrude, calling everywhere for her. But it was no use. The river was still high and flowing fast. He could only think that she had been swept away in the floods and drowned. He was filled with a sense of hopeless despair and wretchedness. He longed to tell his mother, but of course he could not.
He dared not even show his feelings.

In the evening Aunty Gertrude arrived, for it was Christmas Eve. A tree was brought in and together they decorated it before joining the carol singers in the village. But Charlie's heart was not in any of it. He went to bed and fell asleep without even putting his stocking out.

But when he awoke on Christmas morning the first thing he noticed was his stocking standing stiff as a sentry by his bedside table. Intrigued and suddenly excited, he felt to see what was inside the stocking. All he found was a tangerine and a piece of long, stiff card. He pulled out the card and looked at it. On it was written:

To Charlie, from Father Christmas:
Goosey Goosey Gander, where shall I wander?
From the orchard to the fishing hut,
From the fishing hut to the hay-barn . . .

It was clearly his
mother's handwriting.
Charlie tiptoed
downstairs in his dressing gown,
slipped on his wellingtons and
then ran out across the back yard
to the hay-barn.

He unlatched the little wooden door
and stepped inside. In the farthest corner,
penned up against a wall of hay were two tall
geese that cackled and hissed at his approach.

44

They sidled away together into the hay, their heads almost touching. Charlie crept closer. One was a splendid grey goose he had never seen before. But the other looked distinctly familiar. And when she stretched out her white wings, there could be no doubt that this was Gertrude.

But his attention was drawn to a beautifully decorated card, which read:

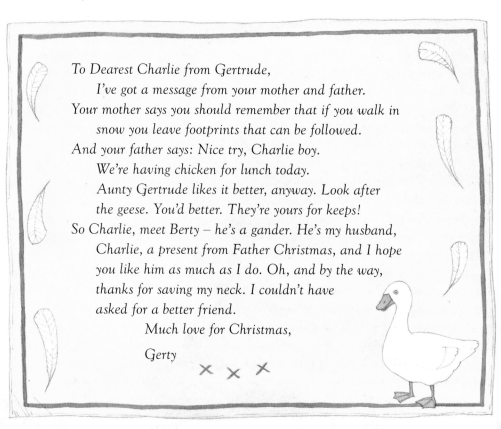

To Dearest Charlie from Gertrude,
 I've got a message from your mother and father.
Your mother says you should remember that if you walk in
  snow you leave footprints that can be followed.
And your father says: Nice try, Charlie boy.
  We're having chicken for lunch today.
  Aunty Gertrude likes it better, anyway. Look after
  the geese. You'd better. They're yours for keeps!
So Charlie, meet Berty – he's a gander. He's my husband,
  Charlie, a present from Father Christmas, and I hope
  you like him as much as I do. Oh, and by the way,
  thanks for saving my neck. I couldn't have
  asked for a better friend.
       Much love for Christmas,
       Gerty
          x x x

By the time Charlie got back to the house, everyone was sitting down in the kitchen and having breakfast. Aunty Gertrude wished him a Happy Christmas and asked him what he'd had in his stocking. "A goose, Aunty," he said, smiling. "And a tangerine!"

Charlie looked at his mother and then at his father. Both were trying hard not to laugh.

"Happy Christmas, Charlie boy, any sign of Gertrude yet?" his father asked.

"Yes," said Charlie, swallowing his excitement. "Father Christmas found her and brought her back – and Berty too – her husband, you know. Nice of him, wasn't it?"

"Gertrude?" said Aunt Gertrude, looking bewildered. "A goose in your stocking?" She looked over her nose just like a certain goose. "I don't understand. What's all this about?"

"Later, dear," said Charlie's mother, gently patting her sister's arm. "I'll tell you about it later, after we've eaten our Christmas dinner!"